HERMELIN

the Detective Mouse

Mini Grey

Alfred A. Knopf ✦ New York

Well, I was trying out
the new binoculars
that I'd found in my
breakfast cereal
that morning.

I'd better
introduce myself.

I am Hermelin.

The first thing I can
remember is waking up
in my cheese box (which smelled

delicious) and finding
I could read the name on it.

It said:

HERMELIN

So I knew

that was what

I was called.

READY SALTED

Then I found this attic.
It is at the top of
Number 33 Offley Street.

It is full of
books and boxes
and boots,
and also
a typewriter.

Well, it was just after lunchtime on Offley Street,
and I was passing the OFFLEY STREET NOTICE BOARD,
and I had a good look at it.

OFFLEY STREET

LOST BAG
It belongs to Mrs. Mattison. Black leather containing life savings.
Tel: 0207 946 0265

GONE!
Have you seen my TeDDY BoBo? He is maybe Lost. TeLL Imogen SpLotts.

Desperately Seeking
PARSLEY
Greenish fur. Distinguished meow
Partial to fish. Greatly missed.
Reports to Captain Potts, 31 Offley

Missing!
My reading glasses have disappeared. If found, notify Dr. Parker at No. 25

DISAPPEARED!
MY BELOVED GOLDFISH
LUCKY
IS GONE FROM HIS BOWL
Any sightings, contact Bernardo Bosher at
BOSHER'S SAUSAGE SHOP
37 OFFLEY STREET

TELECOM

NOTICES

MAN
WiTH
AN
L Andy
00900843

VANISHED!
My priceless Diamond Bracelet
is LOST (perhaps stolen)

GENEROUS REWARD
No Questions Asked
Contact Lady Chumley-Plumley

Have you seen
my notebook?
I would really like it back –
contains vital information.
Emily
at No. 33
P.S. To whoever is
eating my cornflakes –
Help yourself!

I thought to myself:

Great
heavens!

Just LOOK
at all these
lost things!

THESE

POOR PEOPLE

OF

OFFLEY STREET

NEED

SOME

HELP!

And I knew
I was exactly the one
for the job.

So I got to work.

I dropped a note onto
Imogen Splotts's pillow...

Potts

Dear Young Imogen Splotts,

Bobo your Bear has crash-landed
in the lemon meringue pie
that Captain Potts has left out
to cool. He may well be sticky,
but he will smell nice.
                    Yours,
                    Hermelin

Dear Bernardo,
LUCKY, your beloved goldfish,
is currently in
Lady Chumley-Plumley's
        fountain,
being cruelly taunted
by Parsley the cat.
I'd hurry if I were you!
                Yours,
                Hermelin

...and taped another to
Bernardo Bosher's
empty goldfish bowl...

THE DRAMATIC RESCUE OF BABY McMUMBO

It is Thursday,
which is Trash Day
on Offley Street,
and I am
just on my way
to return
a lost notebook
I have found
(to Emily at Number 33)
when I see:

Baby McMumbo has
crawled out of a
front window and
has plopped
into a soft bed
of garbage.

goo!

I must help!

The garbage truck
is getting nearer!

Monday
It looks like my
cereal is being
nibbled—and no
free gift
again!

GARBAGE GOBBLER

There's no time to type,
but maybe I can
use the notebook.

I struggle with the stubby
pencil; my paws are not good
at this sort of thing.

FOLD

FOLD

When the message is written,
I fold it as quick as I can . . .

. . . into an airplane shape
that will fly well,

and with the last of my strength,
I hurl the plane toward
Mr. McMumbo's open window . . .

...where it splash-lands into Mr. McMumbo's Crunchy Flakes.
STOP!
MUNCH-U-LATOR
goo!
DEAR McMUMBOS
PLEASE HURRY
BABY McMUMBO
is in trash AND
in PeriL!
Hermelin
Oval Fruits

Mr. McMumbo just manages to reach the Munch-u-lator Automatic Garbage Gobbler in time.

MUNCH-U-LATOR

gooo!

OFFLEY TIMES

DRAMATIC RESCUE OF BABY McMUMBO

Small child grabbed from Gobbler at last minute

From our Roving Reporter Emily

...y Morning we saw an
...scue on Offley Street.
...mbo, who had been
...eakfast toast near a
...umber 35 Offley
...er-wobbled and
...t of the window,
...seemed- in the
...lled garbage can.

...CAN

...hat Thursday,
...in dire peril,
...or Automatic
...n its way to
...of the bins
...umbo was
...bowl of
...aware of
...earance.

...eries of
...terious
...s have
...ough
...rm-
...or
...en
...t

BUT WHO, EXACTLY, IS HERMELIN?

Then suddenly, with a splash of milk,
an aerodynamically folded note landed
in his cereal. The note read:
"DEAR McMUMBOS PLEASE HURRY
BABY McMUMBO IS IN TRASH
AND IN PERIL! HERME...
The paper it was written on w...
similar to my own lost n...
just as Baby ...d
from the tras...
and was just ab...
from the jaws of the...

...his is just the...
...scues prom...
...ermelin. A t...
...returned
...elin's he...
... completel...
...unicates o...
...iving v...
...e o...

This is jus...
rescues pr...
Hermelin. ...
been returned
Hermelin's he...
...elin is comple...
...communicates...
...note, giving vit...
...helps the owner...
...retrieve their pre...
...The first found obj...
...Mrs. Mattison's ha...
...gone missing on M...
...causing great cons...
...it contained all of Mrs...
...life savings.

MISSING I...
MYSTERIOU...
RETURN...

Mrs. Matti...

...ing handbag

DO YOU SU...
from
...MO...

INVITATION

Dear Hermelin,

We don't know who you are, but you have helped everybody – and you have saved the life of Baby McMumbo.

Please come to a

THANK-YOU PARTY IN YOUR HONOR

at Bosher's sausage Shop
at 4pm this afternoon.

Everybody wants to meet you!

Yours gratefully,
The People of
Offley Street

I spent some time
in my attic
smartening up
my fur.

HERMELIN

BRILLCREME

KITTY CHUNKS

CHIPOLATA FLAVOR

KITTY CHUNKS

KITTY CHUNKS

TOAD in the HOLE FLAVOR

CUMBERLAND FLAVOR

INGRED
PORK
PEPPE
CUMBE
BREAD
LARD

HOORAY HERMELIN THANK YOU FO

Bravo
Hermelin

Quite a crowd
had gathered in
Bosher's sausage shop.

RMELIN

WITH ALL THE
GOODNESS OF SAUSAGE

KITT CHUN

HOT DOG
FLAVOR

I felt very nervous
but took a deep breath
and stepped forward to say
Hello.

MOUSE!

There was a
blood-freezing
scream

and a
rushing
of feet.

Things were
knocked
over and
I was very
nearly
injured.

A Mouse. But what's so bad about being a mouse?

572

mourn
mourn (mōrn) *v.i.* & *t.* Feel sorrow or regret (*for* or *over* dead person, lost thing, loss, misfortune, etc.)
mousaka or **moussaka** /mooh'sahkə/ *noun* a Greek dish consisting of layers of minced lamb or other meat, aubergine, tomato, and cheese with a cheese or savoury custard topping. [Modern Greek *mousakas* from Turkish *musakka*]

mouse. (*pl.* **mice**)
1a small rodent infesting houses etc.; with a pointed snout, and a long slender almost hairless tail: family Muridae.
The House Mouse (Mus Musculus) has been carried around the world by Man.
This **pest** causes **untold damage** annually to foods and materials.

heart   intestines
lungs

House mouse: mus musculus Famil
Mice may carry bacteria, viruses a

L. *mūs*, Gr. *mūs*, Skr. *mūs*;
'**steal, rob**'

573   mouse

play cat and mouse with, torment with suspense;
mouse ~'trap, for catching mice;
mouse ~'trap cheese, of poor quality; timid shy person; **mou'sy̆**
2. (*or* ~z) *v.i.* (Of cat, owl, etc.) hunt mice.
3. (*pl. also* **mouses**) in computing, a small box,

with a movable ball under it, that is connected to a computer and that, when moved across a desk or mat, causes a cursor to move across a VDU screen, so enabling the operator to point to and execute commands.
Albinos - white mice - are valuable research animals.

See also:
PESTS AND DISEASES

moustache
mous'tache, **mus~,
(mŭs'tahsh) *n.* Hair on either side (usu. in *pl.*) or both sides of (usu. man's) upper lip.

MOUSTACHE. The hair on a man upper lip when allowed to grow.

I ran
for my life,
leaving a trail
of crumbs and
cream behind me.

Back in my attic
I consulted the encyclopedia.
Unclean, Unhygienic, Unwanted.
The devastating truth was . . .

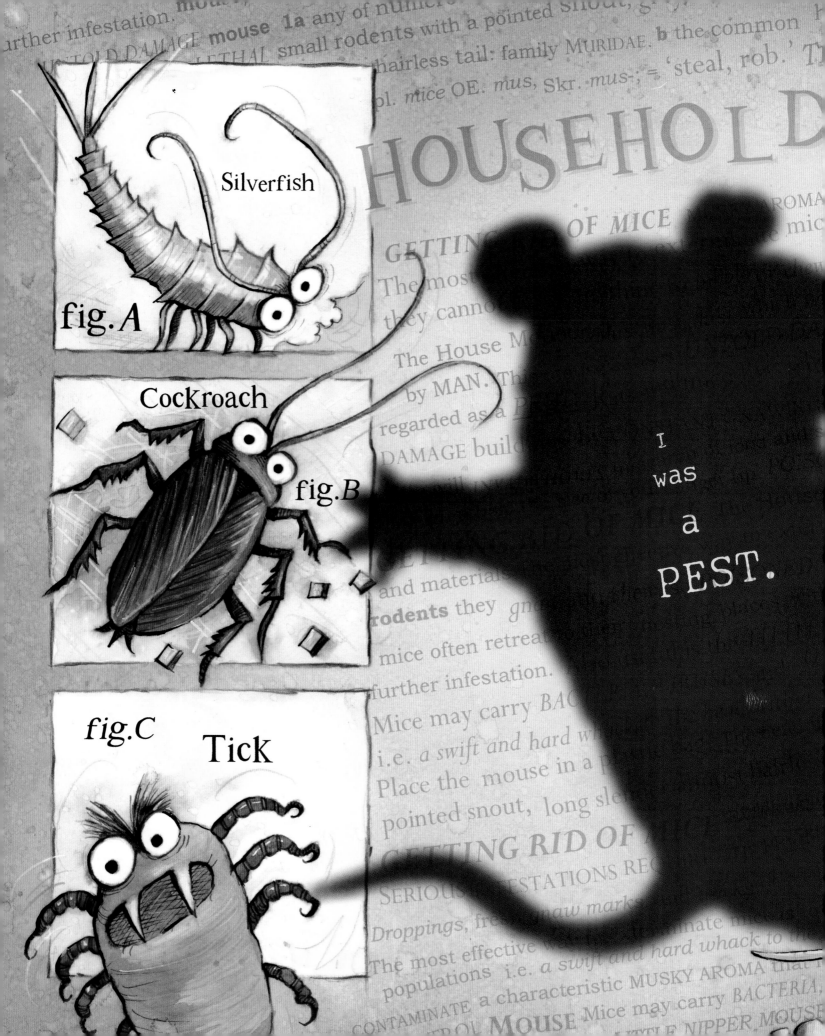

I felt suddenly very alone.
It was time to leave
Offley Street.

I packed up
some things
to take with me
in the morning . . .

and then
sadly went to
sleep in my cheese box.

But while I was

sleeping,

someone found me.

Someone who had

followed

the trail of

crumbs and cream

that led up

the steps to

her very own attic.

And that someone

had a good look around,

Detective mouse needed with good typing skills.

Could you be the one I'm looking for? If so, come down to breakfast with me – Emily I'm waiting!

and then took out
a mouse-sized note
and tucked it
into my cheese box.

And now I have breakfast
every day in the kitchen
downstairs at Number 33
with Emily
(who says she is
a bit of a detective, too).

We read the cereal boxes
and the newspaper, and

we hunt carefully for clues,

because we have a plan
to start a
DETECTIVE AGENCY...

TIMES
PAGE LATEST
RANGE
SAPPEARANCES
MYSTERIOUS ABDUCTIONS
OF LOCAL PETS

Growler   Bonzo   Mr Big   Parsley   "Tiddles"

Missing!

Hermelin & Emily
PRIVATE
INVESTIGATORS
You name it – we can solve it!

. . . as Emily suspects there are
still a few mysteries to be solved
around Offley Street.